CHRISTMAS RIDER

CHRISTMAS Rider

A LOST SAXONS SHORT STORY

JESSICA AMES

Copyright © 2019 by Jessica Ames

www.jessicaamesauthor.com

Christmas Rider is a work of fiction. Names, places, characters and incidents are a product of the author's imagination and are fictitious. Any resemblance to actual persons, living or dead, events or establishments is solely coincidental.

Editing by Charisse Sayers

Proofreading by Gem's Precise Proofreads

Cover design by Desire Premade Covers by Jessica Ames

Cover image copyright © 2019

Please note this book contains material aimed at an adult audience, including sex, violence and bad language.

This book is licensed for your personal enjoyment. It may not be re-sold or given away to other people. If you would like to share this book with another person, please purchase an additional copy for each recipient. If you are reading this book and did not purchase it, or if it was not purchased for use only, then you should return it to the seller and please purchase your own copy.

All rights reserved. Except as permitted under Copyright Act 1911 and the Copyright Act 1988, no part of this publication may be reproduced, distributed or transmitted in any form or by any means, or stored in a database or retrieval system, without the prior express, written consent of the author.

This book is covered under the United Kingdom's Copyright Laws. For more information visit: www.gov.uk/copyright/overview.

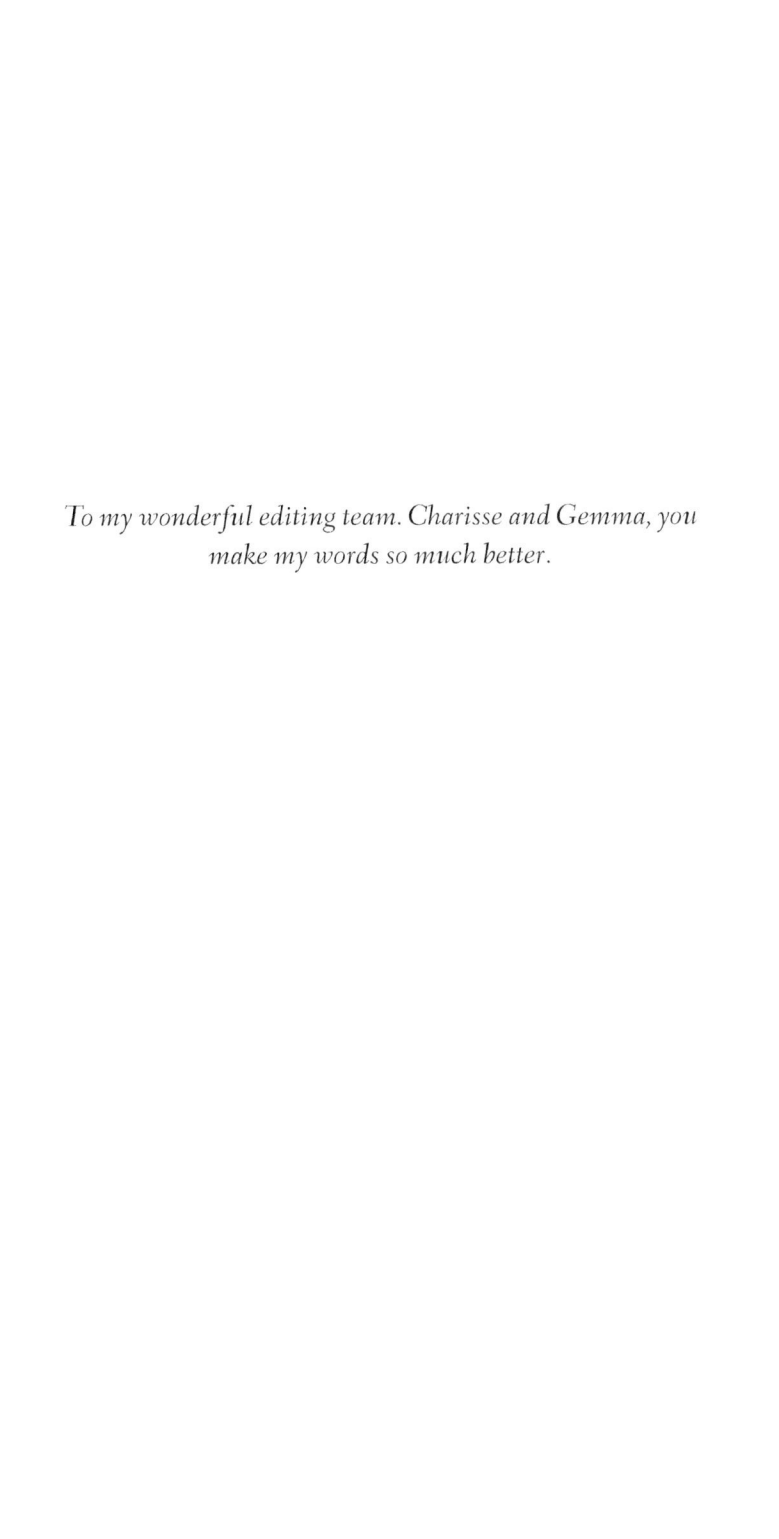

To my wonderful editing team. Charisse and Gemma, you make my words so much better.

CHAPTER ONE

LIV

NINE DAYS UNTIL CHRISTMAS...

"Do you think it'll snow?" I hook the curtain aside with a finger and peer out into the dark night.

The street outside is silent, but that's no surprise. We live on a quiet road. I suspect we're the troublemakers, in fact. Dean is always rumbling up and down the cul-de-sac on his bike, and there's an endless stream of rough and ready bikers turning up at all times of the day and night. Our neighbours must hate us.

"I don't know, darlin'. I hope not. You're ready to have the baby any day now and I really don't want to navigate to the hospital through snowdrifts."

It's less than a fortnight to Christmas, and while the weather has turned chillier, I'm not sure it's cold enough to snow. I wish it would. I love the stuff, and a white Christmas is always magical, but Dean is probably right. The UK isn't really set up for adverse weather conditions, and snow makes everyone drive like the apocalypse is chasing them.

I glance over my shoulder at Dean, who is sprawled on the sofa, in a pair of sweats and a tee, his bare feet leaning on the edge of the coffee table. We were watching a movie, but I had to get up and move around. The joys of carrying a behemoth baby in my belly is that he or she seems to sit on my spine in a way that makes everything south of my hips ache.

I'm so over being pregnant. Don't get me wrong, I can't wait to meet my baby, but I'm done with the whole process of growing the kid. It feels like I've been carrying this baby around for a year, never mind nine months. My feet are swollen to the size of an elephant's and my body aches in ways I can't even begin to describe, and I feel like a whale. I don't have one of those cute, neat baby bumps. I'm all belly, and there's yards of it.

"Well, you want to be a hands-on dad. What's more hands-on than delivering your own progeny?"

His eyes narrow. "Liv, I'm not delivering our kid in the fucking living room."

"Good, because I want an epidural, which I'm certain you can't give me."

I run a hand over the swell of my stomach as the baby gives me a swift boot in the ribs.

Ow, baby, go easy. I've got organs in there I need to keep us both breathing.

"Is she moving?" Dean asks, coming off the sofa and meeting me at the window. His hand cups my stomach and his face goes a little distant.

"Moving? *He's* playing football in there." Dean is convinced the baby is a girl. I like to tease him by contradicting him, although, secretly, I think I'm having a boy. I don't know why, but it's just a feeling I have. I'm probably wrong, but who knows. The little bugger was hiding during the twenty-week scan, so we're in the dark. I was disappointed at the time, but now I'm glad we don't know. I feel more excited about the birth, well, as excited as I can be about pushing a watermelon sized object out of my hoohar.

When the baby kicks me again, a look of pure bliss crosses his expression and his hands move on my stomach to get a better position. He dips his head slightly and says, "Come on, kid, cut your mum some slack."

I get a little giddy at him talking to our baby. He does this often and it's adorable. He's going to be a great father, which I know is something he worries about, given his own father has been locked up since Dean was seven.

"I don't think he cares about slack, Dean. He's out of space in there."

And he or she must be. My due date was three days ago. With all the stuff going down with Piper, Wade's little sister, I haven't had much time to worry about the baby's late arrival. In truth, I was more concerned if she was okay. She was snatched out of her loft in Manchester and held captive for days before Jem and the boys managed to find her. She seems good—as good as someone can be after being abducted.

"I'm not keen on leaving you tomorrow," he admits. "What if you go into labour?"

I'm overdue, so there's every chance that could happen, but this kiddo seems determined to stay snug as a bug inside me. I don't think he or she is going anywhere yet, and this visit is important to Dean.

I glance at the Christmas tree, standing in the corner of the room, the lights twinkling off the tinsel. "It's Christmas, Dean. You have to go."

He does. His father needs to see him.

"But darlin'—"

I place my finger on his lips. "He's your dad, and you do this trip before Christmas every year. That's not changing because you're with me."

His brow draws together. "How do you know that?"

"Your gran told me." Selling Dorothy out is probably not a nice thing to do, but I can't lie to Dean either. We don't have secrets between us, unless it's Club business, but I'm okay with that.

Dean lets out an irritated huff. "She had no right to put that on you, Liv."

I wrap my arms around him and try to hug him—an achievement with two feet of belly between us. Even so, I manage to snuggle my face into his chest and when his hands go around me, I let go of some of my tension.

"She didn't put anything on me. She just asked if you were planning on going." I fist my fingers into his tee and glance up at him. God, he's so handsome. The copper flecks in his beard catch the light and I run my fingers over the hair. "Dean, I'm pregnant, but I'm not made of glass. You don't need to protect me from everything."

"No," his voice rumbles through my cheek, "but everything that's happened lately makes me want to bundle you up and get the fuck out of town."

I know what he means. Between ex-husbands and what Tap and Dylan did, things have been on edge. Then Piper got abducted and everything went to hell in a handbasket. We were locked down at the clubhouse while the boys were off searching for her, but I still felt anxious. I was worried about her, about the boys who went after her, about Dean having to step up and protect his family. I was just worried full stop. It was a relief when Piper came home, although it didn't alleviate any of the fear. Dylan is still out there and things feel just as unsettled as before.

"We can't leave town. Everyone we love is here."

"Right now, the only priority I have is you. You're pregnant. You don't need any stress."

"Well good thing I'm not stressed, isn't it?" I poke him in the side and he twitches away, grabbing my wrist and bringing my fingers to his mouth to kiss.

"I still don't think it's a good idea to go."

"You're going. Even if I have to go with you."

His snort tells me that's not happening. I stare at him a moment, my mind working overtime, and I don't like the ugly feeling that creeps through me.

"Dean, am I ever going to meet your father?"

Is he embarrassed by me? Ashamed? We've been together nearly a year now and I've yet to meet his dad.

He surprises me by stepping out of my hold, his hands rubbing the back of his neck. Ice claws up my spine, as I cradle my stomach, unsure what is going through his head. He's never been standoffish with me before. This new side of him is a little scary.

"No," he says softly after a moment.

I bite on my bottom lip, pulling it between my teeth as pain lances through my chest.

"Are you... am I not good enough for you?" I surprise myself by asking the question and with such defiance in my tone. I'm a long way from the woman who snuck out of Simon's house and fled to Kingsley. I would never have dared to question Simon, but Dean... Dean makes me feel safe to question, to ask, to demand answers, which is why his current attitude is freaking me out.

At least, until his head whips in my direction and he snaps out a "What?"

"Well, I can only assume that's the issue. You never talk to me about him and you never take me with you on visits."

"Yeah, for good fucking reason, Liv. Jail isn't exactly a great place, and where my dad is isn't nice. You're pregnant."

"I'm well aware of that fact, Dean."

"I don't want you in that fucking place. Everything in my life is contaminated by filth, but not you. Never you. Going there puts you in my filth, darlin'."

I stare at him, unsure what he's talking about. "I don't understand," I admit.

I watch as he drags his fingers through the long sides of his hair. It's shaved underneath, but he's growing it longer on top.

"You've never asked about Dad. You're not curious?"

I am, more than curious, I'm downright intrigued about what Dean's father did that landed him in jail with no chance of parole, but I'm not going to probe into Dean's life. He goes once a month to see his father, and when I asked about going with him, he shut me down. I don't know why, but I didn't push it either. We all have shitty pasts to deal with. Dean's no different.

"I figured you'd tell me when you were ready."

He sinks onto the edge of the sofa, his thighs parting to make way for his clasped hands. I want to go to him, but I figure this is a time I need to give him space.

"Dad's doing two consecutive life sentences for killing two police officers."

I try to keep my face blank at his words. I figured he was inside for something bad, given he's been locked up since Dean was seven, but I didn't realise it was this bad. Bile climbs up my throat.

"He beat them to death with a hammer, and because of his Club affiliation, the Judge threw the book at him. He's never getting out."

That information hits me in the gut. I knew there was violence in the Club, but I never realised how much.

"Okay..." I wince. That's sounds terrible. "Dean, it doesn't change anything for me, but he's still your father. You obviously care about him a great deal, so I want to meet him."

"He killed those fuckers for a reason, Liv." He grinds his teeth. "My mum died when I was a couple of months old. She was..." He steels himself before he says, "raped and dumped in a ditch outside of town. Dad tried to find out what happened to her, but he could never get to the bottom of it."

Cold fills me as the pieces of the puzzle start to fall into place, and I'm not sure I like where they're falling. Two dead policemen killed with an unbridled rage, and a raped wife... it doesn't take a genius to figure out what happened.

I can't bear it any longer. I go to him, standing in front of him. I'd love to kneel but there's no way in hell I can get down on the floor with my ginormous baby bump in the way. He doesn't touch me, but I run my fingers through his hair, needing to feel him, needing to touch him.

"Dean, you don't have to tell me."

"Yeah, darlin', I do. I should have told you before now, but it's not easy to talk about."

I can understand that.

Finally, he reaches out and loops an arm around my waist, his face pressing lightly against my stomach.

"Dad couldn't get to the bottom of shit because of who did it. Pigs protect their own and they shut down all investigations. Slade helped Dad get the information he needed, but it took him years." His fingers trace lightly over my hip.

"It was the police officers?"

"Yeah, beautiful. It's hard to be mad at your dad for leaving you when he gave up everything to right a wrong."

It makes warped sense in my mind, but I can't help but feel his dad would have been better placed raising his son. I keep this to myself.

"I love you," I tell him. "And I still want to meet your father."

"Babe—"

"No, Dean. He's important to you, which makes him important to me."

He mulls this over and says, "When the baby's born, I'll take you with me on a visit."

I lean over and kiss the top of his head. "Okay."

"Okay," he repeats.

CHAPTER TWO

BETH

NINE DAYS UNTIL CHRISTMAS...

I STARE at the pregnancy test, my mind racing. Three minutes. Three minutes I have to wait to see if I'm pregnant.

Shit.

Don't get me wrong, I want babies with Logan, but now isn't exactly the best time. My business is just getting started, Dylan is still roaming free and planning fuck knows what, there's a P.I. out there who is determined to get answers about Simon Wilson's disappearance, and my grandfather is not doing well after his pneumonia. Added to all this is the small issue of Slade killing Tap and Jem planning a coup to oust Slade that involves my husband. So, yeah... I'm not thrilled about the prospect of bringing a kid into this mess, but I might not have a choice. If I'm pregnant, then we're having a baby. Lo and I are in a position to have a child and to do right by a kid—even if neither of us is exactly ready.

We weren't trying to get pregnant, not at all, but with the wedding and then Piper going missing, my schedule was all over the place. I guess I must have messed up somewhere and took my pill wrong or forgot to take a dose. That's the only thing I can think, but considering how much me and Logan shag, I guess it was inevitable we'd have a mishap somewhere.

Fuck, shit, bollocks!

My stomach roils and I'm not sure if it's nerves or the nausea that has been dogging my steps all week. I haven't vomited, but I've been close a couple of times. I chalked it up to anxiety at first. Everything was going to hell. Piper was snatched, her friend Cami was brought to the clubhouse looking like she went several rounds in the ring with a block of cement and Jem, Adam, Wade and Weed were out there doing everything they could to bring her home safely.

Yeah, my nerves were shot.

Once everything calmed down, and Piper came home, the nausea didn't abate. I figured I should probably do a test and check. The last thing I want to do is spend the entire Christmas holiday drinking if I'm knocked-up.

I close my eyes and grip the edge of the basin. I swear this is the longest three minutes of my life. They need to make these tests work faster. My heart is pounding.

A baby...

Hell's bells.

Am I ready? Is Logan ready? I don't know. We've barely had time to think since the wedding. Piper was taken the day we got hitched, her friend, Cami, turning up the morning after to tell us she'd been snatched. Everything after that was a whirlwind of activity. The whole Club was locked down while the boys went to recover her.

Was it too much to expect a little less drama now that everything has calmed back down?

"Babe?"

Fuck. Logan's voice drifting through the door has me scrambling for the test. Why? I don't know. If I'm pregnant, he's going to find out. Even so, I yell out, "I'll be out in a second."

"You okay?"

I can understand why he'd ask this. I sound on the verge of hysterics. Why, I don't know. Logan will be happy, I know he will. He's wanted kids since we got back together. I want them too, but I did think we'd have a little more time together before we added to our little family.

Get a grip, B. It's a baby, not a bomb.

A bang on the bathroom door has me jumping. "B? You okay in there?"

"Uh, yeah."

"You don't sound okay. Open the door."

I should open it, because he needs to do this with me. He's as much a part of this as I am, and I don't want to deny him the chance to be involved.

Placing the test on the edge of the sink, I move to the door and pull it open.

Lo is leaning against the frame, looking handsome, as always. His dark hair is rumpled, from his helmet, no doubt, and it curls a little at the nape of his neck. His dark brown eyes appraise me for a moment, seeking any sign of what has me rattled.

"Everything okay?"

Deciding to just rip the plaster off quickly, I say, "I'm doing a pregnancy test."

He stares at me a beat then says, "What?"

"A test. I think I'm pregnant. I've been feeling sick all

week and I missed my period. Well, I didn't miss it exactly, but I'm late, and I'm not usually late, but—"

His finger comes to my lips, and I stop rambling.

"You're pregnant?"

"I don't know. I'm waiting for it to finish... doing whatever it's doing. It's taking a gazillion years. Do you want to come and see what it says? The wait is kind of killing me."

His shocked expression morphs into a grin. "Yeah, darlin', I want to see."

I take his hand in mine, curling my fingers around his and he moves closer to me, cupping my face.

"I love you, B."

"I love you too."

He searches my face for a moment, looking for what, I don't know, then he kisses me softly. I melt against him, needing to feel him, needing the safety of his arms, and he gives it to me, enclosing me in his grip.

For a moment, we just stand locked in each other's hold. I suck up all his warmth, all his reassurance, smell the leather of his kutte and his aftershave.

He kisses the top of my head and says, "Come on, darlin'. Let's go look."

Having Logan by my side gives me the strength to walk back into the bathroom and to the test, which is still sitting on the edge of the basin, where I left it. He massages my shoulder as I tip the test towards me and stare at the little window.

Is that... is that a line? I knew I should have paid that little bit extra for the digital version of this thing. I grab the leaflet and quickly flip through to the part about what the symbol in the window means. A plus means I'm pregnant. I slide my eyes back to the test and the line is forming fast now, becoming solider by the second until the definitive outline of a plus sign is clear.

"Well?" Lo asks. "What's the verdict?"

My stomach flip-flops.

"I guess I'm not doing any drinking over Christmas."

I'm pregnant. Holy shit. I'm *pregnant*.

I brush my hair back and blow out a breath, then I press a hand to my belly and let my lips curve into a smile.

I'm having a baby. I take a couple more deep inhalations, then glance up at Logan, who has the leaflet in his hand now.

"You're pregnant?"

"According to the test, yeah. I mean, I guess I need the doctor to confirm it, but—"

He doesn't let me finish. His brings my lips to meet his mouth and then he devours me. His tongue seeks entrance and I give it to him, even as his fingers go under my top, skimming over my back in a way that makes my muscles quiver. He pulls back, breathless, his forehead resting against mine.

"Are you good with this?"

"Yeah, honey, I'm good."

"You wanted to wait, though. This isn't exactly waiting, love. We were married a month ago."

I did want to wait, but I'm pregnant now. "Plans adapt, Lo. You're okay with this?"

"Yeah, babe, more than okay. We definitely need to look into moving now. The flat isn't big enough for us and a kid."

He's not wrong. The space is good, don't get me wrong, but by the time we got the Christmas tree in the living room, it shrank it to the size of a postage stamp. Plus, we need a garden. I want somewhere safe for our kid to play.

Fuck... a kid.

"Best Christmas present ever," he tells me.

"It's nine days until Christmas," I point out.

"It's the best early Christmas present ever, then."

This, right here, is everything I ever wanted with Logan—the house, the ring and now the baby. I feel warmth spread through me. Things couldn't be more perfect.

CHAPTER THREE

WADE

EIGHT DAYS UNTIL CHRISTMAS...

"Why do we need a tree again?" I demand, watching as Paige unwraps yet another box of baubles. I don't understand the desire to put ornaments on a plastic tree, but Paige was insistent we have decorations. It's apparently tradition.

"Because, Captain Grumpy Pants, it's Christmas."

She's obsessed with this phrase.

My brows climb up my forehead. "Captain what?"

She turns to me, her hands going to her hips in a way that has my dick twitching. I love when she gets haughty. She looks like a naughty vixen.

"It's Christmas, Wade. It's a time when people do stupid shit like putting up a tree and being jolly. Embrace it."

"I am jolly."

Her eyes roll. "You're absolutely the antithesis of jolly."

I have no idea what this means, but I gather it's not a compliment. My retort is shattered when she starts to climb on the edge of the sofa, leaning dangerously to reach the top section of the tree.

I move fast, my hands circling her waist as she wobbles a little.

"Are you crazy?" I demand, lifting her back onto the floor.

"Wade! What are you doing? I need to reach the top of the tree."

"Yeah, not by climbing it like a cat. Tell me where you need this to go and I'll put it up for you."

My desire to protect her always takes me by surprise, but it shouldn't. Paige is my world. I'll do anything to keep her safe—even if it is just putting cheap trinkets on a fake tree. Before Paige, I never had this, although I'm developing this same overprotective streak for my little sister. When she was taken, I swear I was ready to rip the world apart to find her, but I didn't expect her to have another champion.

Things have been good between us for the past few weeks, even with all the strain of my sister being snatched and finding out she's been hooking up with motormouth, Jem Harlow. As loath as I am to admit it, he's good for her. She seems a lot less uptight, and she smiles more. She also moved here, which, I'm not going to lie, makes me happy as fuck. I hated her being so far away.

"I can do things for myself, you know?" she grumbles.

I lean forward and kiss her softly. "I know, but you fall and I'll be upset, so, let me help."

"Fine. I need all these placed around the top of the tree. I'll decorate the bottom while you do that."

"Okay."

"How's Piper doing? I haven't seen her all week."

Paige asking about my sister fills me with warmth. I'm

glad they get on. It makes my life easier, and it's nice to see them bonding.

"She's bruised up, but she seems better. Jem said there's been a few nightmares, but that's to be expected."

Merrick and his bunch of thugs got their comeuppance for touching my sister. She may not have agreed, but she was Club property the moment she got in that car with Charlie and came to sit at my bedside while I was in the hospital. Taking her was a declaration of war, which is why we didn't leave any of his guys breathing at the factory where they were holding her. I wanted to burn the place to the ground, and if we'd had time, I would have, but concern for Piper meant we got out of there fast.

Paige pauses, a bauble clutched in her hand. "Maybe I'll see if she feels up to lunch or something tomorrow."

I squeeze her hip, letting her know how much I appreciate this. "That would be good, sweetheart."

"I adore your sister, Wade. It's hardly a chore."

"Unlike the fucking Christmas nightmare we're engaged in right now."

The glare she fires in my direction is adorable. "Christmas is not a nightmare. Besides, if you want to see a nightmare visit your sister and Jem's place. Cami said it's like Santa puked up in there."

"Jem's a saint, clearly."

She smacks me in the gut. "It makes her happy, and he'll do whatever he needs to in order to keep her smiling. I think it's cute. They're cute together."

My hand comes up. "Don't. She's my sister and I might have to hurt Jem if you continue."

"Are you two boys okay now?"

She means after our little throwdown. We both smacked the shit out of each other until Piper broke it up.

"Yeah, just about. I'm still pissed they both lied, but I get why they did." Kind of. I wish Piper had just been honest with me and not scared to tell me the truth, but Jem's insight into my little sister had me re-evaluating everything. Her parents seem like a piece of work. I feel better knowing she's not embroiled with them any longer.

"Babe, you've got to let it go."

"I have."

Her eyes roll. "Actually let it go, not just say you have."

"I've let it go," I assure her.

She rolls to her toes and kisses the stubble on the side of my cheek. "Good. They're family. We don't hold grudges against family."

I want to point out that she doesn't talk to her own, and Piper is the only member of mine I keep in contact with, but I'm not sure that will keep her Christmas cheer in place. Instead, I lean down and capture her mouth. She leans into me, her body melting against me as I deepen the kiss. Having Paige is my favourite pastime. I love this woman with everything I have, and it pains me to know that Dylan hurt her when I exposed him as a traitor. It makes me want to rip his fucking head off.

This is part of the reason I'm considering getting my scars covered with a new tattoo. I hate that she has such a visible reminder on my body of all that darkness. She wasn't on the scene when I got shot by Tap, but I know she looks at those scars and remembers the aftermath, which involved her getting roughed up by Dylan. Dane, who is the Devil's Dogs VP, is my usual go-to guy for ink, so I'll have to see what he says once they're healed a little more.

My thoughts dissipate when she leans against me, pressing her pelvis to mine. My dick instantly starts to harden. Fuck, this woman. She's everything to me. I'd die to protect her.

Needing her, needing to feel her beneath me, I tangle my fingers in her hair and take her down onto the sofa, still keeping my lips locked to hers. I need to be inside her, now, but I need to get her nice and worked up first. Her sweater pushed up to her chin, I pull her tits free of her bra and suck her left nipple into my mouth before moving to the right. She shifts beneath me, catching my groin as she does and I let out a carnal groan.

She drives me crazy, in all the right ways, and I show her for the next hour precisely just how much.

CHAPTER FOUR

PIPER

SEVEN DAYS UNTIL CHRISTMAS…

THE CLUBHOUSE IS busy tonight and the mood is jovial. For a bunch of men who claim not to like Christmas, they're certainly doing a lot of drinking in the name of the festive season. I don't know where they put it all and how they stay standing after putting it wherever it goes. I can drink a considerable amount, thanks to years of drinking at social events for my parents, but these boys make me look positively lightweight.

Still, I'm not one to give up easily, so I order another G and T and carry it back over to the table where Jem is sitting with his little brother, Adam. He's the quietest of the three Harlow boys. He reminds me of Logan, with that brooding mysteriousness that begs to be explored.

Unlike Weed, who is making a beeline for our table, a goofy grin on his face. I brace, unsure what the man is going to do. Before Jem and I became public knowledge, he would flirt outrageously with me, and given how glazed he looks right now, he might have forgotten I'm not on the market. Jem will punch him—sozzled or not.

He doesn't come to me, though. He grabs Adam around the neck and plants a huge sloppy kiss on the side of his cheek.

Adam takes this in his stride, clearly used to Weed's shenanigans.

"Merry fucking season's greetings." His eyes are heavy, sitting at half-mast.

"How drunk are you?" Jem asks, amusement in his tone.

His mouth moves into a sloppy grin. "Sober enough to realise you're still an ugly bastard."

I snort, I can't help it, but his eyes zero in on me. "Lovely, Piper. If you ever get bored of this fuck nugget, I'm available."

He sinks into the chair next to Adam, barely managing to find it, and reaches for the nearest pint on the table, never mind the fact it's Adam's drink.

"Thank you for that stunning offer," I say, trying to avoid the beer on his breath, which could knock out a buffalo, "but I think I'll pass. I'm very happy with Jem."

"Don't you have girls lining up at the door?" Jem asks. "A string of harems at your behest?"

"Too many to count," Weed admits.

"Then why in the fuck are you creeping on my girl?"

Weed gives an exaggerated shift of his shoulders. "It's amusing. You arseholes are all 'beat my chest' about your women." He slams a fist against his sternum to prove his point.

"There's no one special in your life, Weed?" I ask, genuinely curious about the man.

"Just his right hand," Adam says around a smirk, sounding more like his older brother than is safe.

"You're one to talk," Weed smacks him on the bicep.

"Are you boys planning on putting up a Christmas tree in here?" I ask, peering around the common room. There isn't a hint of tinsel anywhere.

Adam snorts. "If you decorate the clubhouse like you did yours and Jem's place, Derek will pitch a fit."

"It isn't that bad—"

"It looks like a grotto," Weed interrupts.

"It's Christmas. It's supposed to," I counter.

It's also taking my mind off being held captive by that lunatic, Merrick. Those memories are still as fresh now as they were when it first happened.

As if sensing where my thoughts have gone, Jem squeezes my leg.

"Come on, angel. Let's get out of here."

He stands, holding his hand out to me and I take it, letting him pull me to my feet.

"Goodnight, Adam. Weed."

"Night, Piper."

"Yeah, night girl," Weed says.

It takes us a while to leave the clubhouse. Mainly because there's so many people around to say night to, then we head out into the car park. The cold air hits me immediately, and Jem pulls me into his side, sharing his heat with me. And he is warm. He's like a giant radiator.

"We didn't have to leave, Jem," I tell him as we approach the car. I'm too sore to ride, so he borrowed a vehicle from one of the Club's garages—I think the Moor Street one.

"As much as I love watching Weed off his face, I'd rather spend time with you."

This makes my stomach fill with warmth. "You would?"

He moves closer and cups my face in his hands. "Yeah, angel. You're far more interesting than Weed."

He kisses me hard, wet and long, until I'm a panting mess.

"Let's get you home, Pip."

Home. I love how that sounds and I love having my home with Jem. He's fast become my entire life, and I don't care how that might look to outsiders. He takes care of me like no one else in my life, except for Cami, has.

"What *are* we doing for Christmas, Jem?" I ask as we both climb into the car.

We haven't really spoken about it. I feel a little like I'm crashing his plans, considering my move here was last minute.

"What do you want to do?"

"Well, what do you usually do?"

"We all get together and have breakfast at Mum's before heading over to the clubhouse to drink ourselves stupid the rest of the day and night, but if you don't feel like doing that we can stay home."

I know his entire family, so sitting down with them isn't a terrifying prospect to me. "Okay, so we're going to your mum's for breakfast and then the clubhouse."

He glances at me. "Angel…"

"You're not changing your plans because of me, Jem. Besides, it's not like I have any desire to spend the holidays with my parents."

I really don't, considering it was Grant's fault I got abducted and my mother sided with him. I have no inclination to spend time with either of them ever again. Maybe in time, I might cool down, but I doubt it. I had to debase myself to peeing in front of complete strangers because of

Grant. I'm not sure I can forgive or forget that. Not to mention the fact he threatened both me and Cami.

He squeezes my thigh. "Okay then."

"I love you, Jem. I don't know if I say it enough, but I do."

"You could always say it a few more times. Just so the message sinks in. Why don't you start by listing all my best qualities?"

I roll my eyes at him. "Just drive."

"But—"

"Jem..." I lean over the centre console and press a kiss to his mouth, silencing him. His fingers instantly collar my neck, tangling in the hair there. Kissing Jem makes my body quiver and I wish we were home, so he could take me.

When we come apart, we're both a little breathless.

"I need you inside me," I tell him.

He turns to the steering wheel and flicks the key. "You just want me for my body. I feel so used."

The man is like a kid. "Absolutely, now get us home, so I can have my way with you."

He grins. "There's an offer I can't refuse."

CHAPTER FIVE

BETH

SIX DAYS UNTIL CHRISTMAS...

The air is bitter today. I'm glad to be inside my office, cosy and warm. Logan isn't so keen on me being here alone, after what happened with Mr William Brosen, but we haven't seen him since the day he cornered me in the office. I don't know if that's a positive or a negative, but I'm glad he's no longer around. The last thing we need is a private investigator poking about. Simon Wilson is dead, of that I have no doubt. Brosen, and the police, can't prove anything, but I still don't like it. I do not want any of the guys in jail because of that nosey bastard. It sounds cold, but Wilson got what he deserved, completely. He hurt Liv and Dean. He nearly killed me. He shot Wade.

Yeah... he got his comeuppance. If Liv had lost that baby—a baby she's about a nanosecond from giving birth to...

My hand flutters down to my own stomach where mine and Logan's baby is nestled. We haven't told anyone yet. It's bad luck, right? And we have enough bad luck of our own without adding any more. Besides, I still need to have it confirmed by the doctor later this week. My nausea hasn't really abated, but I don't feel so anxious, now I know what is causing it.

"You want a coffee?"

Jamie startles me as she pops her head around the door. Holy crap, my heart is racing. I forgot she was here.

After Brosen's visit, Logan was insistent I had someone else in the office. Jamie was at a loose end, so I offered her a position. She's doing admin duties at the moment, but if she works out, I'll mentor her in the marketing side. I like keeping things in the family, with people I trust.

She also put up the small fibre optic Christmas tree in the corner and some tinsel around both our computer screens.

"Uh—" I do want coffee, but I'm not sure I'm supposed to drink it. I should have done more research... "No, I'm fine."

Her brows pull together. I'm not surprised. I usually can't start my day without a good dose of caffeine.

"Are you still sick?"

"Yeah, I feel nauseous. It's probably not a good idea to drink anything, unless you want to see it projectile vomited across the office."

Her red hair dances around her jawline. "Nope. I'm not sure puke clean-up is in my job description."

It most certainly isn't, and I wouldn't expect her to clean up my mess anyway.

"Did you organise the paperwork for the Dravon file?"

"Yep. It's in your in-tray."

I'll admit, I've been impressed with her work ethic so far. She comes across as a bit of a wild child at times, but she's worked hard for me so far. She's polite on the phone, good with clients, and it's nice having someone here with me. It did get a little lonely before.

"Did you hear about the Christmas dinner?"

"Yeah. Are you going?" Lo goes to his mother's for breakfast with the rest of his siblings, then does his own thing the rest of the day. I don't think he's eaten a Christmas dinner since he lived with his mum. It's a good idea planning a Club sit down meal, but I do worry about the reason for it. Piper, it seems, has become fixated on Christmas since her ordeal. I don't know if it's just a way for her to avoid thinking about what she went through or if she genuinely loves Christmas, but she's like the Ghost of Christmas fudging Cheer. Derek wouldn't let her go crazy decorating the clubhouse, but Lo said he did allow a tree to go up in the corner behind the pool tables. I think it was enough to placate her, and not enough to piss the guys off.

"I don't know. It's a family thing."

"Which you're a part of, J. You're as much family as I am."

She shifts her shoulders. "I guess."

"No guessing. You are. You have Saxons blood in your veins. That makes you family."

I don't know why she has a hard time with this, but I've noticed she's saying more things like this lately.

"Yeah…" she studies me for a moment, then says, "Are you okay, B? You seem a little… strange."

"I'm fine," I assure her, making a mental note to be 'less strange'. "I just have a lot to do before we go off for Christmas."

Jamie studies me, then says, "You're knocked-up, aren't you?"

Heat rises in my cheeks. "What?"

"Girl, in all the time I've known you, you've always had

a huge steaming cup of coffee to start the day. You need it or you're like a bear with a sore head. This morning, you don't want coffee, which makes me wonder why. Then there's the vomiting without any other sign of illness. I might not have finished high school, but I'm not a dunce. I can put two and two together."

I lean my hands on my desk and let my shoulders sag. Considering she's around me eight hours a day, it's going to be difficult to keep this from her. "No one else knows yet, and I'd rather it stay that way 'til we get the all-clear from the doctor that everything is okay with the baby."

A huge grin crosses her face. "Oh my God! I knew you were knocked-up. Your tits look bigger! I thought I was imagining it."

I stare at her a beat, then say, "You're a nut."

"Yeah, but you still love me."

"Yeah, girl, I do." I eye her. "Not a word, though, J, I mean it."

She pretends to zip her mouth shut. "I can keep a secret."

I doubt this, given her personality, but I don't say it. "Thank you."

"Was Lo pleased?" she asks, moving into the room and sinking onto the chair in front of my desk.

Reclaiming my own chair, I smile softly. "Yeah, he was thrilled."

"He's going to be a hell of a daddy."

"I think so too." I have no doubt Logan will make an amazing father. He had enough practice with his own siblings growing up. He pretty much stepped up after Frank died to help his mother with the little ones.

"Between you and Liv, it's enough to make a bitch broody."

"You want kids?" I ask, a little surprised. She doesn't strike me as the settle down type. Jamie is a party girl. She spends most of her free time at the clubhouse, hanging with the boys and making her way through hangarounds. Not that there's anything wrong with that. She's happy and that's all I care about, but babies didn't seem like something that was high on her agenda.

Her shoulders shift, making her hair bob around her shoulders. "Someday maybe. Yeah, I'd like a family. I guess it'd have to be with the right guy, though. I want what you girls have."

Her wistful words make my stomach clench. Jamie lost her father, Jeff, who was a Club member from the time I was young. He and Tap were inseparable. Now they're both gone—Jeff in a brawl, Tap because of his betrayal.

"You'll find him. The perfect guy sneaks up on you when you least expect it."

"I sure as fuck hope so. I'm not really into the whole 'spending my golden years alone' thing."

"Things between me and Logan are good now, but that wasn't always the case, honey. Things haven't always been plain sailing between us."

She waves this off. "Yeah, but you guys are happy little clams now."

I smile. "Yeah, we are."

Work passes by quickly and at six, Lo buzzes the bell at the bottom of the stairs to come up. Jamie heads down to unlock the door and while I wait butterflies flutter in my stomach. He always makes me feel like that, which is something I never experienced with my ex, Alistair.

When he comes into the room, he seems to suck all the space out with his huge frame.

"I'll just be a second," I tell him, itching to go to him, but wanting to shut down my computer, so we can leave.

"I'm heading out," Jamie says. "See you two tomorrow."

"How're you getting home?" Logan demands, his SAA hat always firmly on his head.

"Driving..."

"I'll follow you back."

"Logan—"

His hand comes up. "Don't argue with me. Dylan and that fucker, Brosen, are still out there. You don't go anywhere without an escort."

"I can't wait around for your boys every time I need to do something, Lo." She sounds irritated. I understand it, but when you've had bad things happen to you, you're also grateful for the protection.

"You can, and you will. I mean it Jamie. I find out you've been running around town without a prospect or a brother, I'm going to be pissed."

Her eyes roll. "I'm not scared of you."

His menacing growl and the flinch she gives suggests otherwise.

"Okay, Sasquatch," I say to Logan, "let's just calm things down." I glance at Jamie. "Go and grab your stuff, so we can head out."

She goes, grumbling under her breath about bossy fucking bikers. I almost laugh, but the look on Logan's face stops me.

"She's going to get herself hurt if she doesn't start following the fucking rules. Charlie said she slipped him twice last week."

I rub a hand up his arm, soothing him. "This escorting business is not easy," I tell him. "Cut her some slack. We're all feeling it."

"It's for your own safety."

"We know that, which is why we're all adhering to it, but it's not fun having to wait an hour for a prospect to turn up when all you need to do is nip to the corner shop. And it's invasive. Jamie's a free spirit. She's not used to being followed around."

He leans down and kisses me. "It won't be forever, but it is necessary. We have no idea what Dylan will do."

"I know, babe. Believe me I know, and I have no intention of risking my life." My hand goes to my stomach and his eyes follow.

"Fuck! I want nothing more than to get you the hell out of this shit storm."

I stroke a hand over his face. "This is our family, Lo. We have to stay and be strong for them."

"Yeah, darlin', it doesn't make it easy, though."

"No, it doesn't, but it is what it is." I roll to the balls of my feet and this time kiss him. "I love you."

"I love you too, Beth."

CHAPTER SIX

LIV

FIVE DAYS UNTIL CHRISTMAS...

A TIGHTENING across my belly wakes me. For a moment, I lie still, trying to pinpoint the reason for my discomfort, but I can't. My stomach feels weird, heavier almost, like all the pressure is between my legs, but it's been feeling a little like that for the past couple of days.

Dean shifts in the bed behind me, drawing me into his arms as he often does when we're sleeping. One arm is draped over my stomach, as if protecting us both and I love when he does it. It makes me feel overwhelming gratitude to have a man who cares so much for me.

For a while, I lie in the dark, just loving the feel of him wrapped around me. Then my stomach muscles clench again. It's uncomfortable, but it doesn't really hurt too much. I'm pretty sure it's a Braxton Hicks contraction, though, it doesn't feel quite like the ones I was having earlier in my pregnancy, and I certainly didn't have the feeling of pressure between my legs.

I try to go back to sleep, but the tightening happens

again. I glance at the digital dial on the alarm clock, the red numbers cutting through the shadows of the room. Ten minutes since the last one.

I lie watching the clock, my hand stroking over my stomach and the next one appears ten minutes out again and it hurts a little more than the last. I debate what to do for a few minutes, but then my anxiety gets the better of me. If I'm in labour, I need Dean awake and keeping me calm.

"Dean?" I say his name whisper soft. "Dean?"

"Hmm...? Darlin'? You okay?" He sounds sleepy and dare I say, adorable, right now. I don't want to wake him so early, but I think I need to.

"I think I'm having contractions."

There's a beat of silence, then he's moving. He pulls out of my grasp and the lamp on the bedside table flickers to life, drowning the room in a soft glow. When he turns to face me, he looks a little freaked. I can tell he's trying to lockdown his emotions, though, so I don't freak too. He doesn't need to worry about me. I feel oddly calm about the whole thing. I can't wait to meet our baby. Truthfully, I never thought I would get to have kids.

"You think or you are?"

"I am. I don't know. They feel different to the Braxton Hicks ones." They hurt a lot more for a start.

"How far apart?"

"About ten minutes or so."

He nods and then leans over and kisses me. "I love you."

I start to answer him when another pain ripples through my stomach. "Ow."

"How far apart now?"

"That one was less than two minutes. I don't understand. Aren't they supposed to countdown in increments?" I worry at my bottom lip. "Maybe this is just another Braxton Hicks, honey."

"Well, you're up and I'm up, so let's go to the hospital and see what the professionals say, yeah?"

I nod and watch as he climbs out of the bed and gently pulls me up into a sitting position.

"Let me find you some clothes."

He quickly crosses the room, brushing his fingers through his hair, and pulls his jeans on before throwing a tee over his head. He then goes to the chest of drawers and starts looking in my side for clothes.

My belly feels hard and my back is aching. In fact, my entire pelvis feels achy.

"What do you want to wear?" he asks.

"Just leggings and a tee is fine."

He comes over with the things I've asked for and starts to help me dress. Like I'm a child, he directs me to put my foot in the leg and the other then he pulls the leggings up just past my knees before the bed gets in the way. He helps me into my bra, although I'm sure that'll be the first thing I lose when I'm in a hospital bed, and then pulls the tee—one of his—over my head.

Just as I'm about to stand, another contraction hits me, this one strong along the base of my spine. It hurts. Okay, it more than hurts, it downright steals my breath.

I grip the edge of the mattress and close my eyes tightly as it rolls through me.

"You okay?" Dean asks, rubbing my thigh as it starts to die down again.

"Yeah," I say, panting a little. If this is just the prelude, I dread to think what the main show will be like.

"You think you can walk to the car?"

"Absolutely." This might be an exaggeration. I'm not sure I can walk to the end of the bed right now.

Dean's hands support me, helping me to my feet. My legs are a little wobbly, so I'm glad he's here, but I manage to stand without any fuss. He eyes me to make sure I'm okay, then he pulls my leggings up my legs, the waistband sitting beneath my enormous baby bump.

I cradle the underside of my stomach as I stand.

I have no idea how I manage to get down the stairs, but somehow I do. We make a brief stop in the living room to put my canvas trainers on and a coat with scarf, then Dean takes me out to the car. Once I'm seated and strapped in, he rushes back into the house and grabs my overnight bag from inside the hallway. We packed everything we might need a few weeks back, which was one of our better ideas. I wouldn't want to wait while Dean was rounding my things up right now.

He climbs in the car and pulls his belt on. Then he turns to me and takes my hand, squeezing it.

"You're going to do amazing, Liv."

Tears prick my eyes. "You can't say things like that—not when I'm emotional."

"It's true. Our kid will be the luckiest kid on the planet having you as their mum." He leans over the console, taking my face in his hands and kisses the side of my head. "Let's go have our baby."

I tried to do as my midwife advised and enjoy my labour. It didn't work. No amount of counting it out, or imagining holding my kid made the process anything but horrific. The pain was intense, unrelenting and savage. If it wasn't for Dean's calming presence and reassurance, I would have fallen apart. When the kid finally pushed out of me, I was a sobbing, sweaty mess, and every inch of my vajayjay burnt with pain.

But when the midwife placed the baby straight on my bare chest, covered in body fluids and gunk, in that moment, I was smitten. I wanted to kiss every inch of my baby and hold him close. I never wanted to be separated from my baby, and my brain was still struggling with the concept of 'my baby'.

Exhausted, I stare down at my son. They cleaned him up, weighed him and took all his statistics before he was brought back to us. Dean and I haven't had him out of our arms since.

He's amazing. I can't believe he's here.

The baby looks up at me with slitted eyes, his forehead wrinkling as he tries to decide whether he's going to cry or just fuss a little, and I don't know how I created something so precious, so beautiful.

"Does baby have a name?" the midwife asks as she enters the room to check on us both.

Dean jumps in immediately with the name we picked if we had a boy. "Oliver."

"*Daniel* Oliver," I amend. Dean never mentioned his father's name as an option, but after hearing his story the other day, I wanted to give him something of his own life in his son—especially since we decided on Oliver in honour of me.

"Liv—"

"No arguments, honey. He's Daniel Oliver Lawler."

He closes his mouth and I see the tears pricking his eyes. "Thank you."

"You don't need to thank me." I rub a finger over my son's head as Dean crowds us both, getting as close as the hospital bed will allow. "I love the name and I love him. How did we make such a cute baby?"

Dean's face softens. "Because he's yours, Liv. He was always going to be adorable."

This makes my stomach dance me because I'm fairly certain I look like hell warmed up right now.

"He's got your colouring, Dean, not mine." And he does. His hair is a dark fuzz, not blonde.

He kisses me. "I'll never let anything touch either of you. I want you to know that, Liv. I'll protect you both with my life. You and him are the most important things to me."

"I love you too." And God help anyone who tries to harm our baby because Dean might be fierce, but I'm lethal when it comes to Danny.

CHAPTER SEVEN

WEED

CHRISTMAS DAY...

WOMEN ARE CRAZY. They're obsessed with babies. They've been gathered around Liv and her sprog for the past hour, just cooing and making silly baby speak at him. I mean, don't get me wrong, the kid is cute, but it is just a baby. They don't do much.

If that's the case, then why do you feel jealous as fuck watching Dean play the doting dad?

I silence that voice in the back of my head. It'll lead places I don't want to go—like to my own fucked up childhood.

Instead, I focus on the room. There's Christmas shit everywhere—presents and wrapping paper. There's even a small tree in the corner of the common room. It looks like an explosion in a grotto, but I guess this is what happens when you let a bunch of women organise Christmas Day festivities.

"What's up with your mug?" Logan demands, taking a sip of his pint.

We just finished our first 'Club Christmas' meal. Piper and the other old ladies arranged it and while it was nice (the food was out of this world), it was all a little too kumbaya for me.

"Nothing."

"Nothing sure as fuck looks like something."

I shrug my shoulders. "I'm peachy, Lo."

In fact, I'm high as a kite, but I keep that to myself. I'm pretty sure Dean will throw a shit fit if I'm baked and around his kid. The guy seems to be on cloud nine, and who can blame him? Family is important. Too bad I never had one.

"Peachy? Are you stoned?"

It's like being caught by Dad when Logan is like this, so I decide to embrace the facts, rather than lie.

"Ding dong, merrily I'm high!" I grin, pushing my dark thoughts aside.

Christmas is always a weird time of the year for me, but I'm feeling it more this year, seeing all my brothers happily settled down and creating their own families outside the Club. I'm jealous, I'll admit it. Their women are good people and strong old ladies. I seem to find whiny hangarounds who don't want me, they just want the property patch.

"Don't go near Danny while you're stoned. Dean'll tear your head off."

"Don't worry, Lo. I'm going to be on best behaviour." I salute him and then push off my stool. "I think I might head to bed. This is too—" I break off, unsure what words to use without being an offensive prick, but Logan seems to understand.

He pats my shoulder. "See you later, brother."

He emphasises the 'brother', telling me clearly we're all

family. I don't know if that pity from him makes me feel better or worse.

I head up to my room in the clubhouse. The urge to get on the road and let it soothe my mood away is overwhelming, but I don't smoke and ride. I unlock the door and step into the darkness before flicking the light on.

The room is basic, bland even, but it's home for now. I got kicked out of my last place. In fact, I've been kicked out of so many places, I'm starting to think I'm blacklisted in Kingsley. I don't know why I go out of my way to make shit hard for myself, but I can't settle anywhere. The Club is the longest I've stayed anywhere, in fact. I thought I might have got itchy feet and moved on by now—gone nomad or patched over—but this is the closest to home I've ever felt. I'll die for my brothers, just as I know they would for me, but I want what they have. I need it.

I sag back onto the bed and stare at the ceiling, my hands pillowed under my head. I'm drifting off when my phone vibrates against my leg. I pull it out and peer at the screen. Unknown number.

I answer, "Yeah?"

"Uh, hey, Weed, it's Jesse."

What the fuck? We have two apprentices working at the garage—Jesse and Miles. Jesse is about as useless as they come. Honestly, I have no idea why Dean hasn't let him go yet. I suspect it's a matter of lack of time to deal with it, and because Lawler is a fucking sucker for second chances. If I was in charge, the little shit would have been gone weeks ago, and I'm not shy about telling him this. It means I'm a little confused why the hell he's calling me.

"What the fuck do you want, kid?"

"Look, I hate to call and normally I wouldn't, but Dean ain't picking up."

That's because Dean is downstairs cooing over his kid. "Okay, so what do you want?"

"I need help."

"What kind of help?"

"The kind where I'm in jail. It wasn't my fault," he adds quickly.

I close my eyes. "Kid... how in the fuck did you end up locked up and it's not your fucking fault?"

"That fucker hit my sister, so I slugged him back. Fuck, Weed, no one touches my sister. Not even him."

The vehemence in his voice surprises me, but I'm struggling to keep up here. He's never mentioned a sister. Then again, we don't do a lot of talking. "Who hit your sister?"

"My arsehole father."

His words send a slither of guilt working through me. The kid is sixteen and I see him five days a week. I had no idea any of this was happening in his life. It sure as fuck explains a lot, though.

Is he being hurt at home?

Is he safe?

I was so focused on his performance I never once stopped and asked the kid about his life.

Flashbacks of my own past roll through my brain on repeat. If someone had stood up for me, helped me, I might never have spent most of my life lost in the system.

"I'll be there in ten with a solicitor. Don't say a fucking word to the pigs. Don't agree to any interviews. Just keep your piehole shut until I can get there, got it?"

"Yeah, Weed," he sounds relieved, *"I got it. And thanks."*

"Don't thank me yet, Jesse. I might not be able to do shit. It's the holidays. People are busy."

"It's okay if you can't..."

"I didn't say I couldn't." I sigh. "Sit tight, yeah?"

"Yeah."

I hang up and immediately hit the number for the Club's legal team. Yeah, it's Christmas Day, but given how much we pay those fuckers to keep them on retainer, they'd best suit up and work their fucking magic. No way am I letting that boy sit in a jail cell over the holidays.

Fuck.

THE END

Did you love reading about the Lost Saxons Motorcycle Club? The story continues in book six: Flawed Rider…

GET A FREE GIFT AND EXCLUSIVE CONTENT

Dear Reader,

Thank you so much for taking the time to read my book. One of my favourite parts of writing is connecting with you. From time to time, I send newsletters with the inside scoop on new releases, special offers and other bits of news relating to my books.

When you sign up, you'll get a free gift.

Find out more here:

www.jessicaamesauthor.com/newsletter

Jess x

ENJOYED THIS BOOK?

Reviews are a vital component in any authors arsenal. It enables us to gain more recognition by bringing the books to the attention of other readers.

If you've enjoyed this book, I would be grateful if you could spend five minutes leaving a review on the book's store page. You can jump right to the page by clicking below:

https://books2read.com/ForbiddenRider

ALSO BY JESSICA AMES

Have you read them all?

IN THE LOST SAXONS SERIES

Snared Rider

A decade ago Beth fled Kingsley for one reason and one reason only: Logan Harlow. Sure, the man is a sex on legs biker, but he's also a thief; he stole her heart and broke it. Now, she's back in town and has no choice but to face him.

Download here: https://books2read.com/SnaredRider

Safe Rider

A new life; a new start—that was what Liv needed after escaping her violent marriage. Moving to Kingsley was a chance to show the world she wasn't defeated by her past. No part of that plan involved falling in love with a biker.

Download here: https://books2read.com/SafeRider

Secret Rider

A one-night stand—that was all she was supposed to be. She wasn't supposed to walk into his bar a week later and demand a job. Wade is used to dealing with formidable women but Paige may just be his match. She's fiery, feisty and he wants her, but before they can be together, he needs to learn what she's hiding.

Download here: https://books2read.com/SecretRider

Claimed Rider

(A Lost Saxons Short Story)

Liv survived a nightmare. She may have got her happily ever after, but things are still not perfect in her world. How can she prove to Dean that she's his in every way that matters?

Download here: https://books2read.com/ClaimedRider

Renewed Rider

Beth knows she has to fix things before her family is destroyed and she knows the only way to do that is with Logan at her side. Together, can they renew the bonds of brotherhood and rebuild the club before it's too late?

Download here: https://books2read.com/RenewedRider

Forbidden Rider

The Lost Saxons stole Piper's future. They took her brother from her, put him on a bike and made him one of their own. Hating them was easy—until she met Jem Harlow. He's irritating beyond belief, pushy, charming, attractive, and he knows it. And he won't leave her alone. Worse still, she's falling for his act. There's only one problem: her brother does not want her anywhere near his club friends.

Download here: https://books2read.com/ForbiddenRider

Christmas Rider

(A Lost Saxons Short Story)

Christmas in Kingsley should be a time for celebration, but with a maniac on the loose and a private investigator dogging their steps, things are tense as the festive season gets underway.

Download here: https://books2read.com/ChristmasRider

STANDALONE BOOKS

Match Me Perfect

He's a fisherman, she's a marketing manager. He lives on an island, she lives in London. Can online dating really match two people from different worlds?

Download here: https://books2read.com/MatchMePerfect

ABOUT THE AUTHOR

Jessica Ames lives in a small market town in the Midlands, England. She lives with her dog and when she's not writing, she's playing with crochet hooks.

For more updates join her readers group on Facebook:
  www.facebook.com/groups/JessicaAmesClubhouse

Subscribe to her newsletter:
  www.jessicaamesauthor.com

- facebook.com/JessicaAmesAuthor
- twitter.com/JessicaAmesAuth
- instagram.com/jessicaamesauthor
- goodreads.com/JessicaAmesAuthor
- bookbub.com/profile/jessica-ames

Printed in Great Britain
by Amazon